Dedicated to the crews and families of the *Scorpion,
Thresher, Kursk*, and good ol' *SSBN-644*.

Manufactured in China by C&C Offset Printing Co. Ltd. Shenzhen,
Guangdong Province, in October 2014

Published by Little Bigfoot, an imprint of Sasquatch Books

19 18 17 16 15   9 8 7 6 5 4 3 2 1

Editor: Susan Roxborough
Project editors: Michelle Hope Anderson and Em Gale
Illustrations: John Skewes
Book design: Mint Design
Book composition: Joyce Hwang

Library of Congress Cataloging-in-Publication Data is available.

ISBN: 978-1-57061-925-0

Sasquatch Books
1904 Third Avenue, Suite 710
Seattle, WA 98101
(206) 467-4300
www.sasquatchbooks.com
custserv@sasquatchbooks.com

This is **Pete.**   This is **Larry.**

Pete has a bucket and shovel to carry.

A day at the beach! What a place to explore!
Could Larry and Pete ask for anything more?

Pete began building
A castle of sand.
Larry thought maybe
He'd give Pete a hand.

But then a strange animal
Crept into view.
A seashell with legs?
This was certainly new!

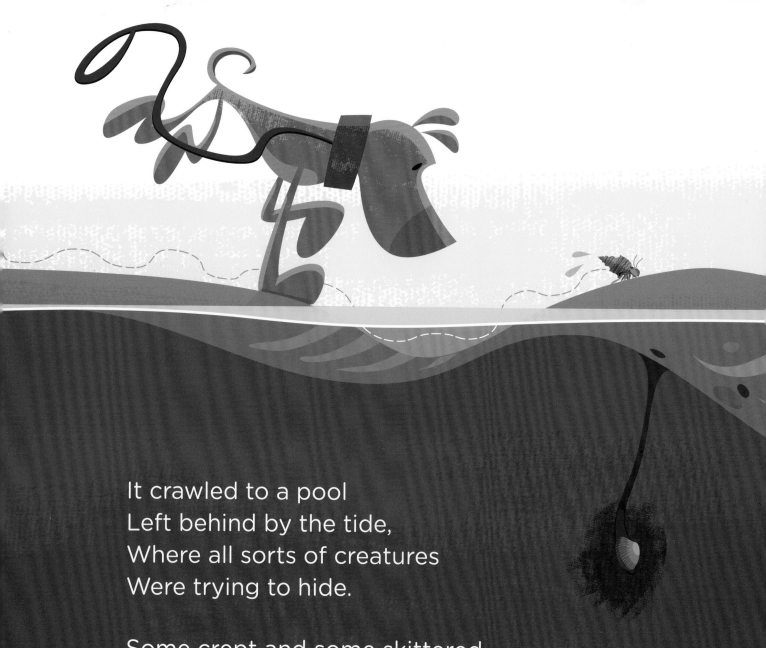

It crawled to a pool
Left behind by the tide,
Where all sorts of creatures
Were trying to hide.

Some crept and some skittered.
Some swam with a flash.
Then suddenly Larry
Was caught by a . . .

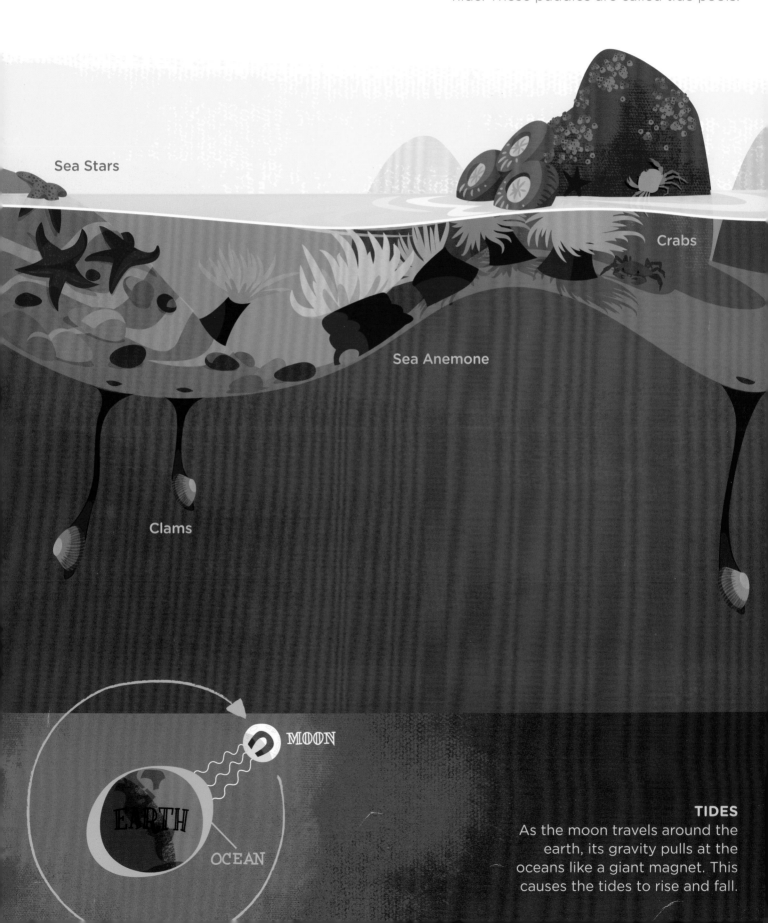

TIDE POOLS
Every day, the ocean tides go in and out, in and out. Puddles of water are left behind, where all sorts of ocean creatures live and hide. These puddles are called tide pools.

Sea Stars

Crabs

Sea Anemone

Clams

MOON

EARTH

OCEAN

TIDES
As the moon travels around the earth, its gravity pulls at the oceans like a giant magnet. This causes the tides to rise and fall.

SPLASH!

Hermit Crab

Barnacles

So Larry set off
In his dog-paddle style.
He might as well swim
And explore for a while.

A garden of plants
Bumped his nose and his knees,
And grew like a forest
Of undersea trees.

Rockfish

SEABIRDS

Most seabirds have dense feathers to help protect them from the ocean water and rain. Beneath the outer feathers is another thick layer of feathers called "down." Down feathers help keep seabirds warm.

Salmon

Surfperch

KELP FOREST

To avoid being eaten, many fish and other sea creatures hide in jungles of tall seaweeds called "kelp forests." Kelp also provides food for some ocean creatures, such as abalone and sea urchins.

Larry dove deeper,
And what should appear?

FISH ANATOMY

Fish don't need scuba gear to breathe underwater. A fish takes water into its mouth and forces the water out through its gills. The gills pull the dissolved oxygen from the water, allowing the fish to breathe. Most fish stay afloat with the help of a swim bladder, like a tiny balloon inside. A fish lets air into its swim bladder when it wants to swim higher and lets air out when it wants to travel deeper.

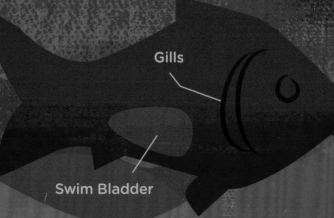

Gills

Swim Bladder

A man in a mask!
What was *he* doing here?

SCUBA
How do divers breathe underwater? They use scuba gear—special hoses attached to tanks filled with air. "Scuba" stands for self-contained underwater breathing apparatus.

The man scooped up Larry
And rose from the water.
What's this he'd discovered?
A walrus? An otter?

They boarded a boat
Where his friends took a look.
They'd never seen "dogfish"
Like *this* in a book.

OCEANOGRAPHER
If you enjoy learning about the sea, you might
grow up to be an oceanographer. Oceanographers
are scientists who explore and study the ocean.

Soon all the workers
Were noisy and busy,
But Larry missed Pete,
And he wondered, **Where is he?**

He snuck down a tunnel,
And as he went creeping,
Suddenly Larry
Heard buzzing and beeping.

That pup tried to hide
To escape the commotion,
But when he looked out . . .

He was under the ocean!

The water was filled
With all sorts of surprises;
Fishes and creatures
Of all shapes and sizes.

SUNLIGHT ZONE

Sea Turtle

Hammerhead
Shark

Jellyfish

Octopus

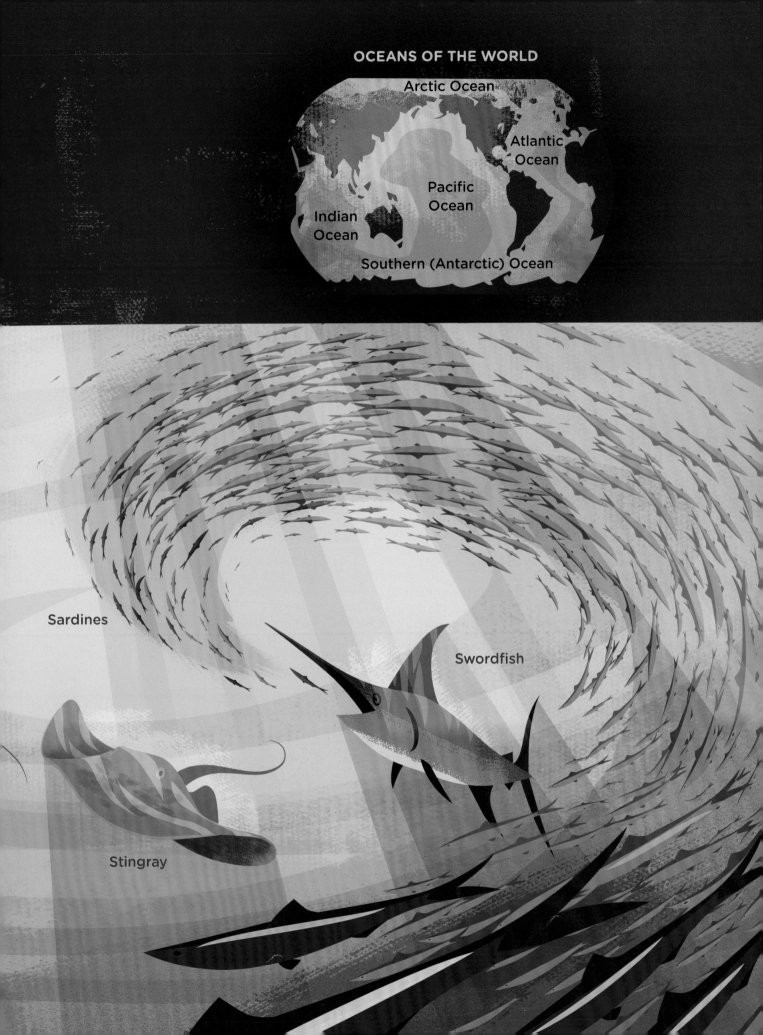

OCEANS OF THE WORLD

Arctic Ocean

Atlantic Ocean

Pacific Ocean

Indian Ocean

Southern (Antarctic) Ocean

Sardines

Swordfish

Stingray

As they went deeper,
The water grew dark.
The sunlight above them
Was barely a spark.

BATHYSCAPHE
When scientists want to explore the deepest parts
of the ocean, they use a bathyscaphe. These special
vessels are designed to travel much deeper than a
diver could ever safely swim.

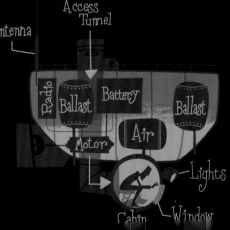

Antenna

Access
Tunnel

Radio

Ballast

Battery

Ballast

Motor

Air

Lights

Cabin

Window

SUNLIGHT ZONE

Spanning from the surface to 656 feet deep, sunlight penetrates the ocean in this zone, and this is where most undersea life lives.

TWILIGHT ZONE

Spanning from 656 to 3,300 feet deep, only a little sunlight is visible in this zone.

MIDNIGHT ZONE

Everything deeper than 3,300 feet—no sunlight reaches this zone. In the complete darkness at this depth, some creatures glow with their own light.

He peeked out again.
What a shock! What a scare!
Creatures like giants
Were swimming out there!

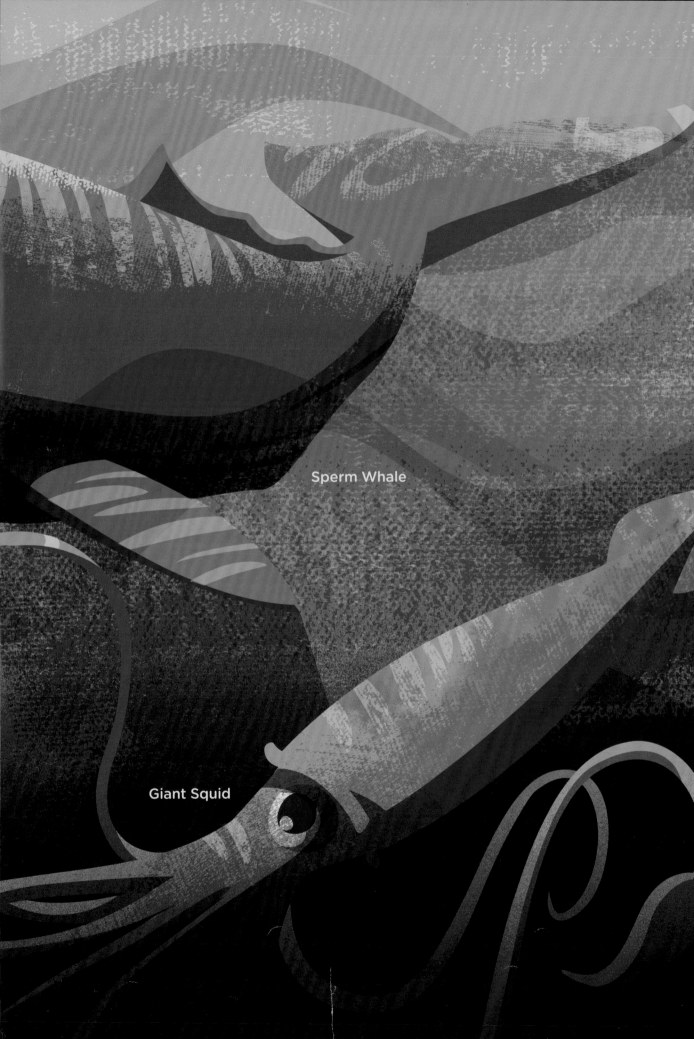

Sperm Whale

Giant Squid

MIDNIGHT ZONE

Humpback
Anglerfish

Darker and darker
The waters were growing.
Larry was worried.
Where could they be going?

Here he saw fish
That flickered with light.
They glimmered and shimmered
Like candles at night.

Hatchetfish

Deeper they traveled.
His eyes opened wider.
Now he saw creatures
That crept like a spider!

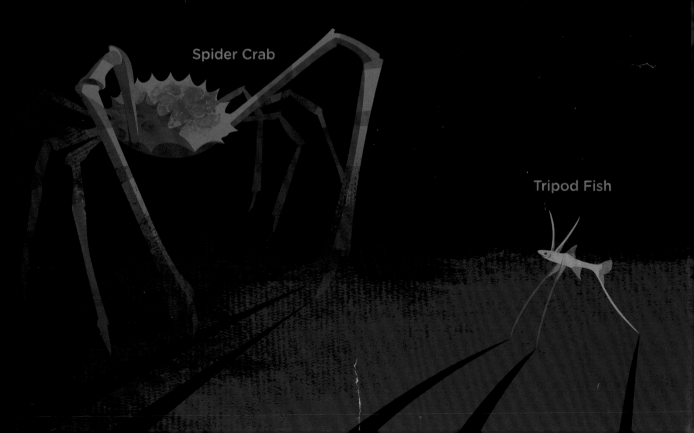

Spider Crab

Tripod Fish

HYDROTHERMAL VENTS

When cold seawater seeps through cracks in the ocean floor, it reaches hot magma deep in the earth. The magma superheats the water, and it boils out like an undersea geyser. Scientists have found strange animals such as tube worms, clams, and crabs living near these vents.

Then hot, steamy bubbles
Rose up in the dark.
Larry grew frightened.
He let out a bark!

Giant Tube
Worms

Vent Crabs

"Well, look who's on board,"
Said the man with a smile.
"Let's get you back home.
We've been gone for a while."

They rose to the surface,
Where he opened a door.
They hopped in a boat
And then raced back to shore.

And soon they were sleeping,
As tired as could be,
Two friends together
With dreams of the sea.

Get More Out of This Book

Group Discussion

» Ask readers to talk about a time when they saw a tide pool. Have them describe the creatures and plants they saw. Then ask readers to think about how a "big splash" from a tidal wave might affect a real dog and a real hermit crab. Talk about which of these two animals would best be suited to stay and live in the water. What adaptations would make that possible?

Group Activity

» Ask readers to reread the caption on page 13 that describes the kelp forest. As a group, draw a food web of other plants and animals that exist in the ocean habitat. Research what the term "symbiotic" means. Include at least one symbiotic relationship in the food web.

Independent Activities

» Reread the caption on page 17 about oceanographers. Write interview questions you might ask someone with this career. Research the kinds of problems oceanographers try to solve.

» Reread the caption on page 22 about the bathyscaphe. Design a machine you could use to explore the ocean. Then, write a brochure that would persuade an oceanographer to buy it.

» Think about the three zones of the ocean mentioned in the book. Then, from memory, sketch some of the animals that live in each zone.

TEACHER'S GUIDE: The above discussion questions and activities are from our teacher's guide, which is aligned to the Common Core State Standards for English Language Arts for Grades K to 4. For the complete guide and a list of the exact standards it aligns with, visit our website: SasquatchBooks.com

Learn More at Your Local Aquarium

WEST COAST

Seattle Aquarium
Seattle, WA

Point Defiance Zoo & Aquarium
Tacoma, WA

Oregon Coast Aquarium
Newport, OR

Steinhart Aquarium
San Francisco, CA

Monterey Bay Aquarium
Monterey, CA

Aquarium of the Pacific
Long Beach, CA

SOUTHWEST

Dallas World Aquarium
Dallas, TX

MIDWEST

Shedd Aquarium
Chicago, IL

SOUTHEAST

Georgia Aquarium
Atlanta, GA

The Florida Aquarium
Tampa, FL

North Carolina Aquarium
Manteo, NC

Ripley's Aquarium
Gatlinburg, TN, and Myrtle Beach, SC

NORTHEAST

National Aquarium
Baltimore, MD

Maritime Aquarium at Norwalk
Norwalk, CT

New York Aquarium
New York City, NY